Bigfoot Sasquatch Files

Volume 4

By Kevin E. Lake

These stories are true.

Potentially...

1

Poached

(Originally Titled: The Unfortunate Demise Of Old Man Singer)

My first runin with Old Man Singer came when I was about twelve years old. My childhood friends and I were sleigh riding on the steep road that ran up the hill leading to Old Man Singer's home. The road was steep, and when it snowed and the road iced over we could fly down it on our steel runners. It was the steepest hollow in our small community. Or, as we pronounced it in Appalachiastan, the steepest *holler*.

"You boys can stop this nonsense right now, or I can call the law on ya. Which is it gonna be?" It was Old Man Singer. He'd pulled over in the wide spot beside the road where we always burned an old car tire to stay warm when we went sleigh riding. (Yes, I hate to admit this all these years later, but we had no idea at the time that we were poisoning the world by doing it. It *was* Appalachiastan). He held a burning cigarette in his hand, and he must have smoked them one right after another, because when he'd rolled down his window to threaten us smoke came barrelling out of it.

"Fuck you, Singer!" my buddy Billy yelled. "You call the law on us, and I'll just tell 'em about that doe I saw you shoot last summer!"

"Them goddamn blades on them goddamn sleds make this road slicker than greased owl shit, you little shit! Now stop, or I'mma call the law!

"Call 'em, you old cocksucker," Billy yelled back. "We'll see who gets wrote up!"

With that, Old Man Singer stuck his cigarette in his mouth and cussed at us a little more while he cranked up the window on his old four wheel drive suburban, and then off he went, up the hollow to his home, and he didn't seem to have any problems getting up the hill despite the fact that we'd been sleigh riding on it for hours. He had chains on his tires, like most of the folks who lived up the hollow. There weren't many houses up there, but if the folks who *did* live up there wanted to get in and out during the winter, they knew to use chains.

"Who was that?" I asked Billy.

"Old Man Singer," he said, like I was supposed to know who Old Man Singer was. Then he spit into the fire. He'd lifted a box of his old man's Skoal again. Sure, I tried it. It made me puke. But not Billy. He loved the stuff.

"Who's Old Man Singer?" I asked, realizing Billy had no intentions of enlightening me further if I didn't.

"The biggest goddamn poacher in the county," Billy said, and yes, twelve year old kids in Appalachiastan really *do* speak that way. Hell, I'm sure twelve year old kids everywhere speak like that when grownups aren't around.

"How do you know?" I asked.

"I seen him kill a doe in his damn front yard last summer," Billy said. "Went home and told Dad, and he said he does it all the time. Everyone knows about it."

"Why don't he get in trouble?" I asked.

"No one gives a shit around here," Billy said, and his answer was sufficient. We lived in a small town in the middle of nowhere in the middle of Appalachiastan. Everyone knew everyone else, and most of the people who lived there were related to each other. The authorities didn't give a shit about a deer or six being killed out of season, especially when it was your third cousin twice removed, and a third time removed again by way of marriage doing the killing.

I'd later ask my father about Old Man Singer, when we were out hunting the following fall, and he filled in a lot of the gaps that Billy had left out.

"He likes to go spotlighting," my father said. Spotlighting is a highly illegal form of deer hunting in which one goes out at night and shines a bright, powerful spotlight out into the fields or into the woods, looking for the eyeshine of deer. Deer, just like when they see headlights from a car, will totally freeze up when they see the spotlight. The hunter, rather, the *poacher*, then shoots the deer while it's just standing there, staring into the light. Last I checked, it's a method that's illegal in all states.

"He'll bury the deer under the snow," my father said, "and then come back and get 'em the next day. Make it look like he killed 'em that morning. That way he doesn't run the risk of the game warden catching him at night.

"He's been known to set out traps, too, which isn't even legal around here," my father continued. "Basically, he hunts year round, and he follows no hunting laws."

"How come he doesn't get in trouble?" I asked.

"No one gives a shit around here," he said. He and Billy were on the same page in that regard.

Years would pass. I'd grow up and leave Appalachiastan. But I remember getting word by way of Billy, now living on the west coast and doing quite well for himself. I promised I wouldn't out him as far as what he's doing, because many of you reading this would know who he is, trust me, but what I will say is he's come a long way since being that cursing and tobacco spitting twelve year old hillbilly kid back in Appalachiastan. He quit chewing years ago, and he never took up smoking or drinking.

"Found him ripped to shreds," Billy told me over the phone when he'd called with the news.

"A bear?" I asked.

"Nope," Billy said.

"What was it?" I asked.

"No one knows," he said.

"Aren't they going to investigate further?" I asked.

"Nope," Billy said.

"Why not?" I asked.

"No one gives a shit around there," he said, and his answer was sufficient, but I went back the following summer and investigated myself. I talked to a few of his family members, and I spoke with the conservation officer who found his body. At least what was *left* of his body. Everyone seemed pretty convinced that a bitch named Karma paid Old Man Singer a visit out in those woods, but no one was convinced Karma had come in the form of a bear. When I pressed harder, and asked about a particular creature that's not supposed to exist, I got doors slammed in my face, but not before being given looks that said, *oh, my God! That's exactly what I thought!*

From the bits and pieces of information I gathered, and from hiking out into the woods where it all went down and searching around myself, this is how I believe Old Man Singer met his unfortunate demise.

***

Old Man Singer had been getting paranoid in his old age. Sure, he'd poached his whole life, just like his daddy before him, and his daddy's daddy before that- poaching was a long running family tradition in the Singer family- and he'd never been caught, but he didn't trust those conservation officers as much as he used to. Too many millennials of age now, filling such job positions, and every damn one of them out to be nice to everyone and everything. Including animals. Hell, Singer thought, if the good Lord hadn't wanted us all eating animals, he would have made them out of styrofoam instead of meat. But those damn millennials. Must all think the meat they eat grows in a garden, Singer thought.

Singer had gotten away from taking his rifles out into the middle of the woods and just blasting away at the wildlife in the middle of summer. He no longer wanted to take the risk of one of those young conservation officers hearing the shots, or have someone else report the shots, so he'd upped his trapping game.

Singer used the most horrific jaw type bear traps in existence, but he didn't use them to trap bears. He used them to trap deer. He'd take a solid number sixteen Duke trap, the springs of which were compressed with more than five hundred pounds of pressure each, and then bury the trap in half a bag of cracked corn. It never took long for a hungry deer to be caught in the trap while feeding on the corn, and once caught, it couldn't free itself. Singer would show up the next day and club the thing to death with a baseball bat he always carried into the woods with him for such purposes. If anyone were to ever ask, he'd claim the bat was for self defense- so many hippies out there smoking pot in the woods these days, he'd tell them, and God knows how violent people get when they're on the marijuanna- but no one ever asked, because no one gave a shit around there, but Singer always had his story ready.

Singer had gone out to check one of his traps on the day of his unfortunate demise. But once he got to the spot where he'd lain it out, it wasn't there. Nor was the corn he'd buried it in. There were a few kernels here and there, so he could tell something had eaten it, but there was absolutely no sign of his trap, whatsoever. Further, there was no sign that maybe a large animal, like a bear, had gotten caught in the trap and managed to walk off, dragging the trap along with it.

Singer got down on his knees and studied the ground where he'd staked the trap's chain. He had pounded the iron rod into the ground pretty deep, but it was gone as well. It looked like someone had simply pried it right up out of the ground and taken it- rod, chain, trap and all.

"Shit!" Singer said, aloud, having a sudden flash of insight. "Goddamn conservation officer got it!" The level of Singer's paranoia reached new heights. "Probably recording me right now on one of them goddamn hidden trail cams!"

Singer stood slowly and looked all around, turning a full circle as he did. First, he looked at ground level, and then he spun a full three sixty and looked at eye level. One more turn, while looking up, and he was convinced there were no cameras and he almost fell down from making himself dizzy.

He badly wanted to pull out a cigarette and light up, but he knew that if one of those millennial bastards were in the woods, waiting on him, he'd give away his position with the scent of the smoke. As hard as it was, he put off the urge to smoke and began slowly, cautiously and paranoidly as hell making his way out of the woods.

He'd only gone a few yards before noticing a pack of cigarettes lying on the forest floor. *Hm*, he thought. *There they are.* He'd had them with him the day before, when he'd come out to set the trap, but he didn't have them when he'd gotten back to his truck. "Must have fallen out of my pocket," he said to himself.

Singer bent over to pick up the box of Newports, and just as he touched the box, the mighty Duke number sixteen jaw trap closed on his forearm, breaking it instantly, the teeth of the trap deeply piercing his skin.

"Ahhhhhhh!" he screamed, and the echoes from his scream bounced back from all the different mountain tops from every different direction all around him.

He never saw what took his head off. He was too busy screaming and being in agonizing pain, but the pain didn't last long, because at least the one hunting him, poaching, rather, as such traps are illegal in the area for any reason, was more humane in regard to a quick kill than Singer had ever been.

But after that? Well, the thing just had fun ripping Singer's limbs off his body, years of rage finally being let loose.

They found the trap with Singer's arm in it two days later. His wife had reported him missing, but only because the Singers were a one vehicle family and she needed to run off the mountain and go to town, but she couldn't very well do that without the truck.

They found one of his legs a couple hundred yards away from his arm and the trap, but the boot had been taken off. The other leg was never found. His torso appeared to have had two giant hands shoved right into it, and his rib cage had been ripped clean open, the same way someone might open a package from Amazon.

The oddest thing of it all, and this is what piqued my curiosity enough to actually go back to Appalachiastan after being gone all these years and investigate this event, was that Old Man Singer's boots were found a few months later, during deer season, by an actual legal deer hunter. They were sitting together, beside a stream, as if someone had simply taken them off to wade in the water. The hunter claimed to have noticed them in the morning when he'd first entered the woods. He left them at the time, assuming their owner was nearby, but when he saw them at the same place on his way out of the woods that evening, he decided to take them with him. Upon doing so, he noticed they were covered in what appeared to be dried blood. He assumed the blood might be from an animal, perhaps killed by another hunter, but he decided to turn the boots into the authorities anyway. As it turned out, they had belonged to Old Man Singer, who had been mangled by someone, or something of great strength almost fifteen miles away the summer before.

Despite the finding of Old Man Singer's boots by the stream nearly fifteen miles away, and despite there being no animal native to the area which possessed the ability to rip a man's limbs off in such a fashion, except for a *really* large black bear, and despite a few pleas from Mrs. Singer to investigate the unfortunate demise of Old Man Singer further, no one ever did.

Because no one gives a shit around there.

The End

2

Sasquatchers Anonymous (SA)

(Originally Titled: The Unfortunate Demise Of Thomas G.)

"You have *got* to be kidding me," Thomas G. said to himself, aloud, reading over the search results he'd pulled up online. "Sasquatchers Anonymous?"

Thomas G. needed a new twelve step program. He was in a new town, in a new state, actually, and it was quite rural where he was, but he'd hoped to find a twelve step program or two where the members were addicted to some sort of substance, be it in chemical or drink form. Those were his niches. They'd *always* been his niches. The niches where he got his bitches, as he referred to the women he met in such programs.

Thomas G. was a shyster, and a shyster of the worst kind. Nay, Thomas G. was a predator, and a predator second only to those who prey on children.

Thomas G. was a registered, licensed, educated, professional and very effective psychologist and drug and alcohol counselor. The problem was, Thomas G. was also a sex addict, and he used his profession to feed his addiction; young beautiful women- and what better time to get them than when they were going through a great time of need in their lives. A time when they were trying to stay alive by overcoming their addiction to drugs or alcohol and sometimes both. And who better to help them through such times than a caring professional who actually had the answers they sought.

Thomas G. had been raised in privilege, being that his father had been very successful and had become very rich working in media after returning home from World War II a hero. It was simpler times, because people still trusted the media, and the media was simply much more trustworthy. After Thomas G.'s mother died while he was still in grade school, his father would marry a woman who went on to become an independently wealthy entrepreneur, having made millions off of her passion and hobby; candle making. She'd developed her own line of scented candles and gave it a quirky name, something that had to do with being a northerner, because Thomas G. and his father were from the south, and in a matter of only a few years, her line of candles went huge and to this day they are burned in many houses across America.

Thomas G.'s stepmother had loved him like her own child and she had spoiled him. With the passing of his mother at such a young age- a woman he loved- and the fine treatment from his stepmother- another woman he loved- he found himself growing up to be a man who truly loved women and who understood it was possible to love more than one- even if at the same time- and thus his course was set. Mommy issues led to sex addiction, and now here he was considering going to a Sasquatchers Anonymous meeting, well, because he wanted to get laid.

Thomas G. had never planned on preying on his patients. He'd never planned on opening an addiction center in order to have an ever ongoing flow of drunk and drugged up women coming in for treatment for him to prey on. He'd never intended to claim to be an alcoholic or addict himself in order to be accepted into all those meetings in order to have a constant pick of new women to prey on.

But he did.

All of it.

Thomas G. had the members of the twelve step groups he'd belonged two convinced that he'd been sober for nearly twenty years. But it all came crashing down on him, hard, when his third wife, half his age and bat shit crazier than the first two bat shit crazy women he'd married relapsed, again, and spilled the beans.

Drunk off her ass, bat shit crazy wife number three went to an open meeting with about fifty members and told of how Thomas G. had been going to meetings, nightly and for nearly twenty years, talking the talk and quoting the program's literature, word for word, and then going home afterward and drinking. No, he didn't always get drunk, but he usually did, and the next day he'd repeat the cycle.

Thomas G. had partnered with three other group members to open a rehab clinic, all three of whom were sober- *really* sober- and part of their pact had been that if any of them were to ever relapse, they had to forfeit their portion of ownership of the clinic to the other, sober members. After bat shit crazy wife number three spilled the beans, Thomas G. found himself without a business.

But hey, he thought. Fuck those t-totalers. He'd just go into private practice, but that only lasted a month before he lost his counselling license, because bat shit crazy wife number three had contacted the state psychiatry board and informed them that Thomas G. was fucking one of his patients; a twenty one year old college student who'd come to him for counselling because she knew that if she didn't get sober and stay sober she'd never graduate. Despite being old enough to be the girl's grandfather, Thomas G. had her pants off in his office on her first visit, and bat shit crazy wife number three, who'd actually been a patient of his when they'd met- very similar circumstances- walked in on her husband and the young coed in action, and the event is what led to bat shit crazy wife number three's relapse in the first place.

Thomas G. hadn't *really* been run out of town on a rail, but he'd been run out of town on a rail. Everyone hated him.

They'd trusted him, accepted him, and they'd all loved him, believing that he suffered from the same deadly illness they did and they'd believed that he'd truly wanted to get it in check and keep it in check. The whole while, though, he'd only been using their programs to find needy women in needy times and using his psychological know how to tell them exactly what he knew they needed to hear, when they needed to hear it, making him appear to be savior like, while the whole time, he'd merely been another thirteenth stepper.

And now here he was, in some shit hole town nestled in the Appalachian Mountains, actually considering going to a Sasquatchers Anonymous meeting to find a needy young woman whom he could mind fuck and then fuck.

"Sasquatchers Anonymous," he said, aloud, again, as if hearing the words again would make it seem any less crazy.

Thomas G. found the group's website, and their program was pretty much mirrored after all the other twelve step programs. The members of Sasquatchers Anonymous all believed they'd seen Bigfoot Sasquatch at some point, and many of them claimed that the experience ruined their lives. They'd been dumb enough to speak of their sighting, publicly, and they'd been rediculed and laughed at ever since. Many of them lost their jobs, having been viewed as mentally unstable. And the worst of it, they'd gotten addicted to going back into the woods, or the desert, or along the beach where they'd seen what may or may not exist, and looking further, hoping for another sighting. Sasquatchers Anonymous had been set up in order to help these people overcome their addiction to going out and looking for the beast that may or may not exist. Return to a normal life. Be able to hold their heads up high in public and look other men and women in the eyes.

"Whatever," Thomas G. said, closing his laptop. He stood and pulled on a light jacket, because it was fall and the temperatures were much cooler at the higher elevations of Appalachiastan than what he was used to down south, and he exited his shitty little roadside no tell motel and he got in his car and headed to the meeting.

***

"My name is Jim R. and I'm powerless over Sasquatch."

The members of the small group, about ten of them, were starting the meeting by introducing themselves and proclaiming themselves to be bonafide members, the only requirement being a desire to stop seeking Bigfoot Sasquatch. Thomas G. could not believe he'd actually come to the meeting. Hell, he couldn't even believe such a group existed.

"And you, Sir?"

"Oh," Thomas G. said, realizing he was being addressed by the group's leader. "My name is Thomas G., and I'm powerless over Sasquatch."

"Thank you," the leader said, and then the introductions continued.

Not only had Thomas G. been preoccupied with disbelief of the existence of such a group, but he had also been preoccupied with checking out the twenty'ish year old blond sitting opposite from him in the circle. When it was her turn to introduce herself, she did so as Jane, and she proclaimed her complete and utter powerlessness over Sasquatch.

"Would you like to start tonight?" the group's leader, Ken R., said to Thomas G. "Since this is your first time here?"

"I think I'd rather just listen tonight," Thomas G. said. "Since it is my first time and all."

"Fair enough," Ken R. Said. "Jane," he then said, turning his attention to the beautiful young blond and only female in the group. "Any more disappearances up your way?"

"Not since my boyfriend. Back in high school. That's been three years now," Jane said.

Mumbles of 'good' and 'um-hum' circulated quietly around the room.

"So it's paid off not to go looking for the creature," Ken R. said.

Thomas G. was staring intently at Jane, and having spent more time in his field than Jane had yet spent on earth, he could clearly make out the signs of frustration on her face. Though she was obviously trying to keep the signs at bay, Thomas took note of the tightening of her jaw, the crinkles around the corners of her mouth and eyes.

"I've never gone looking for them," Jane said, and though she was trying not to sound defensive, she clearly was.

"Now Jane," Ken R. said, trying to sound soothing but failing. "We've talked about this. It's called denial, and until you get brutally honest with yourself, you'll never recover. And we can't do it for you. We can only help you as far as you're willing to help yourself."

Thomas G. saw his opportunity. He'd easily be able to step into Jane's life and fill the void that the people in this program were not filling. Then, he was sure, he'd be able to step into her pants. But first, he needed to know at least a good portion of her story, so he baited her by way of good old fashion passive aggressive fishing.

"I'm Thomas G.," he said. "And I'm powerless of Sasquatch."

"Hi, Thomas G.," the group members said in unison.

"Sorry to chime in," he said, trying not to sound *too* cheesy by using the word 'chime,' the telltale sign of week writers, but marginally acceptable with spoken language. He was intentionally trying to come across as less intelligent as he was. People fear stupid people much less than geniuses. "But I think I can relate."

"How so?" Ken R. asked.

"Well," Thomas G. said. "I've never gone out, actively, seeking this creature, but he, she, it or they continually appear in my life, and I think this group might be able to help me if I could hear some instances of others being sought out, rather than being the seekers."

He'd looked at Jane while he'd spoken, laying the bait right at her feet, and boy, did she ever take it, setting the hook herself in so doing, and then run deep. Thomas G. sat back and listened as Jane basically spent half of the meeting sharing about how she'd first seen two of the creatures when she'd been about four years old. Her daddy, who wasn't actually her daddy, was tuning up on her mommy, and the creatures had helped her sneak out of the old trailer home the family lived in and they took her out into the woods and played with her all day to keep her entertained, away from the drama, and safe.

Jane further shared about times when men, and one high school kid, had tried to harm her in ways unimaginable, and from out of nowhere, Bigfoot Sasquatch would show up and save the day. "They're my guardian angels," she said when she wrapped it up, and Thomas G. knew exactly how to take things from here.

***

Thomas G. tread lightly. He first asked Jane to join him for coffee in a public place, so she would not feel threatened. "There's the gas station down on Main," she said. Thomas G. had forgotten. He was in Appalachiastan now, and there were no coffee shops. "How about the Mountaineer Mart?" he said, suggesting the only other alternative of the shit hole, meth infested town. "Okay," she'd said, and it was on.

Thomas G. attended every Sasquatchers Anonymous meeting held over the course of the next few weeks. Monday, Wednesday and Friday at five o'clock p.m., like clockwork, and he was never late. He respected the group. He was always at least ten minutes early, and on Fridays he went half an hour early to help set up the chairs and make the coffee. And after every meeting, he'd spend time with Jane, usually at the 'meeting after the meeting' in the parking lot, where there were other Bigfoot Sasquatch addicts, so that she would feel safe. But after nearly a month had passed, he decided the time had come to strike.

"You know," Thomas G. said to Jane while they were having coffee in the parking lot of the Mountaineer Mart one Friday after a meeting. "As you know, from our talks, and with all the time we've spent together, I am a licensed psychologist. I think I could help you overcome your Bigfoot Sasquatch addiction if we had a few private sessions. And I'd never dream of taking a dime from you for my services."

"But I've told you, Thomas G.," Jane said in her extremely sensual Appalachian American accent, "I don't go out a'lookin' for 'em. *They* find *me* when I need 'em."

"I know," Thomas G. said. "But maybe just spending some quality time alone for a few therapy sessions could help you in other ways. I know you come from a broken home. A lot of abuse. You just seem to have too much to offer the world not to get out of this shit hole and do something more with your life. Not to mention you're absolutely beautiful."

"Why, Thomas G.," Jane said, batting her eyelashes. "Are you trying to get me to take you home?" And then she smiled, daringly, flirtingly, and completely no way to say no to-ingly.

"Yes!" Thomas G. said. Sure, he was old enough to be this beautiful young woman's grandfather, and he knew it, but it had been so long since he'd lain with a twenty-ish year old girl, the gig was up. He could no longer take it. The time to strike had come!

"That's all well and good, Thomas G.," Jane said. "I ain't got no problem takin' ya back to my trailer, but you gott'a realize, these creatures are empaths. They can sense your true intentions. If you intend to do anything other than try to help me, they'll know, and it won't end well for you."

"It's okay," Thomas G. said, trying to mentally keep his manhood from rising, which it was, and no physical contact had even yet been made. "I can assure you my intentions are," he paused, looking for the right word. "Grandfatherly," he said when it finally came to him.

"Well," Jane said, looking down, a tempting smile on her face. "I never knew who my daddy was. And I sure as shit never knew who my grandaddies were, cause Mamma didn't know who her daddy was either."

Stay down, Thomas G. was mentally telling his manhood. *Stay down. Not yet.*

"Well," Jane finally said, matter of factly. "I reckon it's okay if you follow me out to my trailer. We can talk. I'll take me some of them counsellin' services you're offerin'."

"Lead the way," Thomas G. said, almost running to his car, the only Audi to be found in Appalachiastan.

***

Thomas G. followed Jane, who was driving a beaten, old Chevy S-10- the kind Thomas G. hadn't seen in years- and one that he couldn't believe even passed inspection. But with a smile and an ass like Jane's, Thomas G. figured she probably got just about everything she wanted or needed with little friction, like an inspection sticker for her truck that couldn't pass inspection. The girl had probably never opened a door for herself her entire life.

As they drove up Jane's hollow, pronounced 'holler' by the locals, the day's light grew dim. Evening was here. At least twilight.

The veil was thin.

Just before rounding the last turn and reaching Jane's mobile home, Thomas G. slammed on his brakes as two large, dark figures ran out in front of his car. They'd been fast, and he hadn't been able to make out what they were, but he could tell they were huge.

"Must have been bears," Thomas G. said to himself, massaging the bulge in the crotch of his pants with his left hand. "Bigfoot. Hah! What bullshit."

Thomas G. knew there was no such thing as Bigfoot Sasquatch. Only ignorant hicks, like Jane, believed in such poppycock. Sure, he knew, the girl was hot, but she was nothing more than hillbilly white trash like everyone else from Appalachiastan. They didn't have advanced degrees, from the University of Virginia, at that, like him. He'd decided from the time he first lay eyes on Jane that he'd play along with her silly belief system and her backwoods culture. Just long enough to get in her pants. And he'd continue to play along if he could stay in her pants for a while. But once he saw that he either wasn't going to get in her pants, or that she was going to kick him out of her pants once he'd worn out his welcome, he planned on giving her a good old highfalutin, sophisticated, smartest mother fucker in the room tongue lashing. One that would make her feel even more insecure than she probably already did because of her upbringing.

"Here we are," Jane said. She was standing at her truck when Thomas G. pulled into what passed as her drive, a wide spot beside the road. He'd never been in a mobile home before in his life, but he figured there was a first time for everything.

Thomas G. had played the role of the sophisticated older man for nearly a month now, but he'd massaged the bulging crotch of his jeans a little *too* much on the way up the hollow, and the jig was finally up as far as his acting skills went. He had one thought and one thought only, and that was to have Jane, this beautiful young hillbilly girl, right here, right now.

"Jane," he said, lunging toward her and kissing her. He wrapped his arms around her and nearly came in his pants when he pulled her tightly into him.

"Thomas G.," Jane said, pushing him off. "Now I done told you. You better be careful, or you're a cruisin' for a bruisin'."

"You know that's all bullshit!" Thomas G. said, and then he lunged in for another kiss. He knew she was just playing hard to get. Being a tease. He would call her bluff. He would have her.

Whack!

Something smacked Thomas G. across the back of the head, hard, sending him straight to the ground.

"Goddamn it!" he shouted. He rolled over, and standing over him was something that was not supposed to be real. It was only supposed to exist in urban legends and folklore. Only dumb hillbilly white trash believed in the existence of the kind of shit he was now staring at right in the hairy face.

"No!" Thomas G. screamed out, but it was too late. One powerful swipe from the creature's open hand, its long, sharp claws extended, took Thomas G.'s head clean off of his body.

Jane walked over to Thomas G.'s severed head and picked it up, turning its face toward hers. She'd read (yes, some dumb hillbilly's actually read, and believe it or not, some even write books) somewhere that some guy in France was doing studies on guillotine beheadings centuries ago to see how long a human head remained conscious after the beheading, and she remembered it was something like seventeen seconds.

Jane held the head in her hands and stared into its eyes. She got the distinct feeling that Thomas G. was still conscious. She smiled, and the head smiled back at her.

"Better watch that thirteenth step, Thomas G.," she said. "It's a doozy." And then she lightly kissed the head's mouth and as she did she could feel its lip muscles go limp. She knew that Thomas G.'s head had completely expired.

She lay the head softly on the ground. She stood and turned slowly, and there, before her eyes, was the guardian angel who'd severed Thomas G.'s head from his body and one of its buddies standing only a few feet behind him.

"Well come on, ya'll mother fuckers!" Jane said to them. "Drag this piece of shit's body off and get rid of it like ya'll did all the others!"

Jane walked into her trailer to grab a Miller Lite, and her guardian angels did as she'd instructed. They dragged Thomas G.'s body and carried his head out into the middle of the woods in the middle of Appalachiastan. No one would ever find either. But they made sure to take his shoes off and leave them, together, beside a stream in a very popular hunting location a considerable distance away, where *they* would be found.

Just to fuck with people.

The End

3

Final Vacation

(Originally Titled: The Unfortunate Demise of River Float Karen)

It won't take too long to tell this one, because there's not much to tell, really. Just a story about the very unfortunate demise of a woman we'll call river float Karen. And we won't be capitalizing the words river and float in front of the name Karen, as they should be in order to remain grammatically correct, and not because we're too lazy to hit the shift key too many times, but because we will not dignify her memory by doing so. Karen was *not* nearly as important as she thought she was.

Why river float Karen? Well, because that's what she was doing at the time of her unfortunate demise. She was floating down the river.

And why Karen? Was that her real name? It's possible, but I doubt it. We're calling her Karen here, because she was a typical privileged white woman.

Oh, I'm getting ahead of myself again.

Let's start at the beginning.

So here's the deal. There's a particular spot on a particular river in my community, Charlottesville, Virginia, that is haunted as fuck. The land on both sides of the river used to be part of a massive plantation. Many enslaved people were worked to death, literally, along the banks of the river, and when they dropped dead, their bodies were simply buried in unmarked, shallow graves.

Many years before the land was part of a plantation, it was the living, hunting and warring grounds of many different Native American Indian tribes. Archeologists have found artifacts in the area dating back nearly fifteen thousand years. In a word, there have been a lot of tragic events take place in the area, hence its paranormal activity, and hence, in my opinion, the presence of- and I'm just saying 'potentially' here- Bigfoot Sasquatch.

There is one particular spot on the river, ironically just below its most popular swimming hole, that has always intrigued me the most. The reason why is because I have both fished and kayaked this portion of the river, and every single time that I have, I believe I have seen something, out of the corner of my eyes, watching me. At times from the bank, and one time, from within the water. It was like something large, but not aquatic, was in the water with me, hunkered down with only its eyes and nose above the surface.

Every now and then, my beautiful bride and our son will ask me to take them swimming in this river and at the swimming hole above the bend in the river that I've just described, and I always jump at the opportunity. Not just because I absolutely love doing anything and everything with my wife and our son, but because it gives me an opportunity to go squatching in a place I firmly believe may or may not harbor that which I'm constantly seeking; Bigfoot Sasquatch. One day this past summer we went to the river, and the swimming hole, which we'll call the Bigfoot Sasquatch hole, and this, dear reader, is where we met river float Karen.

I first noticed river float Karen from a distance. My family and I were swimming and playing in the water at the lower end of the Bigfoot Sasquatch hole. It had been my idea, because the position allowed me to peer around the bend where I'd felt like I was being watched so many times in the past. If a Bigfoot Sasquatch were to make its way out of the woods and slip over the bank and into the river, I would be able- potentially, now- to see it while safely keeping an eye on my family as well.

I heard what sounded like squawking. I could tell it wasn't coming from a duck or some other sort of water foul, because it was not a beautiful sound of nature. It was an annoying, bitching and complaining sound of a narcissistic post middle aged white woman. (Hey. We live in Charlottesville. You learn to recognize this sound quite well.) I glanced upstream, and there she was, in all of her two hundred pound plus glory, floating down the river on an innertube that looked like it wanted to commit suicide due to clinical depression induced by having to carry her wait. And not just the weight associated with her body, but the weight associated with her ego.

"Disgusting!" I heard her scream from about two hundred yards away, but I couldn't make out the rest of what she was saying. There were many families swimming in the river that day, as it is probably the most popular river swimming hole in town, and I could see that each time river float Karen got within speaking distance of anyone else in the river, she would speak to them, and every now and then she'd shout the word "disgusting" or "filthy" or "polluted" or "dirty" and then she would keep floating by.

I could tell by the body language and reaction of the people she spoke to that whatever she was saying must not have been very pleasant. Most of the people turned their backs to her and some of them even got out of the river until she passed. One family actually packed up their things and left.

"This should be interesting," I said to my wife, and she just giggled. That's what she does. She giggles. That's why we call her Giggly Girl, but that's another story. But I'll tell you the reason she was giggling at this time, and it's because she knows I don't put up with bullshit. I detest narcissists, and I don't cower to their passive aggressiveness. I call them out.

"Oh, this water looks filthy!" river float Karen said, aiming her bitchery in my direction once she was within speaking range of me. "How can you people be in it?" she asked, looking at me directly now.

Thinking that maybe I'd missed something, I looked around in the water, and just as I'd thought, and just as it has always been, the water was crystal clear. It's the Rivanna River, and it's a heavily protected part of the Chesapeake Bay Watershed, and the water has always been so clean, at least in the twenty years that I've been in the area, that you could drink it. I looked back up at river float Karen just in time for another derogatory statement about the water. "Isn't there sewage in here?" she asked.

"Yes," I said, totally lying. "There's a busted sewage pipe about a mile upstream. I'm actually standing in poop right now." My wife giggled as I said all of this and turned her back to river float Karen so she couldn't see.

"Are you serious?" river float Karen asked, and you could tell that she was serious. She was believing me.

"He's pulling your chain, and you're letting him," a thin man of about Karen's age said. He was floating in an innertube beside her. I'd noticed him, visually, but he'd not been bitching and moaning on his way down the river. As it turned out, the man was river float Karen's husband. We'll call him beta-male, because that's what he was. It was obvious that river float Karen had his balls in a jar somewhere, either hidden in her purse or locked away in a bank box, just in case he ever felt the urge to go searching for them.

"Hey, you," river float Karen said to me. "You better watch it buster, or someone's gonna be calling the cops to report that a teacher shot and killed an unarmed white man." Just the month before, police in Minneapolis had choked George Floyd to death, and just the week before, police in Georgia, I believe, shot and killed an unarmed black man. The nation was being torn apart, at least in the major cities, all over the country by means of violent radical protests as a result. And river float Karen thought this was something worth joking about.

"How is that even remotely funny?" I asked her.

"Oh, come on, you!" she said. "Look at me. I'm a white woman. And I'm a teacher. I belong to a union."

"We're progressive liberals," beta-male chimed in. (And yes, the word "chimed" is a sign of weak writing, and I'm using it here because a weak word goes so well with such a weak man.) "From Montana."

"I think you might not be quite as progressive as you would like to think you are," I said.

"You must be from here," river float Karen said. She'd nailed me as the target she'd been looking for all day, and I was happy to oblige. "Only a southerner would consider this water clean."

"I've been in third world countries where the waterways were so polluted, you could walk across the rivers and be completely supported by the trash on top. You'd never get your feet wet. So to think of this water as filthy is asinine."

"We've vacationed in the Mediteranian," river float Karen said, "where the water is so clear you can see the bottom a hundred feet down."

"Then you should go back to the Mediteranian," I told her. "You should never come here again."

"Oh, we're *not!*" river float Karen said, annunciating the word 'not' so profoundly that she wanted to make it as crystal clear as the waters of the Mediteranian that our community would *never* have the privilege of being blessed with her presence again. "Ever!"

"We won't miss you," I told her. My wife was giggling so hard now Karen noticed.

"Who's that?" Karen asked. "Your daughter?"

"Yes," I said, putting my arm around my wife. "Doesn't she look just like me?"

Okay, so if you don't know me and my wife from our YouTube channel Homesteading Off the Grid, I'll spell it out for you. I'm a white man in my late forties, as of this writing, and my wife is a very beautiful, very petite Filipina lady in her early thirties. In a word, we look *nothing* alike.

"Why are you being so rude to us?" beta-male asked, and he almost made eye contact with me when he did. His voice cracked at the end, as if he were going through puberty, and it's possible he was, as he certainly didn't seem to possess the testicular fortitude that most men actually get after having gone through puberty.

"Because you fuckers want to come to *our* town, float down *our* river, and act like a couple of grasshoppers high on a leaf looking down on all us pissants, and let us know how much better than all of us you are," I said, and both river float Karen and beta-male were speechless. I'm used to this effect. There are a shit ton of privileged narcissists in Charlottesville and none of them are used to being called out on their shit by guys like me, because most people don't call them out on their shit.

I believe the reason there are so many privileged narcissists in Charlottesville is because of two things. Number one, the area is very affluent, and the people here who are *not* affluent want everyone to think they are, so they act like pricks, and number two, it's a college town, so it's filled with intellectual elitist wannabe's. A bunch of educated fools who aren't nearly as smart as they want everyone around them to believe they are. I can tell you, I know many people in Charlottesville who *are* affluent, and I've met many of the people who are extremely intelligent, and what I will tell you is that these people, the ones who are the real deal in both categories, are the salt of the earth. They put on *no* airs, they are humble, and it would blow your mind to know that you'd just talked to a multimillionaire or a scientist in charge of a major pharmaceutical company's research and development lab if you were to speak with them, because of this.

The narcissistic pricks? Like river float Karen and beta-male?

They're fakes!

"Why are you here anyway?" my wife asked. "You're not supposed to cross state lines."

We were at the peak of the coronavirus pandemic. In our state, you had to wear a mask in order to enter any businesses or public buildings. Many states were requiring that people self quarantine for up to two weeks if they were entering from other states. Yet, here was river float Karen and beta-male, self proclaimed progressive liberals from Montana, whatever the hell that means, twelve states away from home.

"Maybe your English isn't that good, sweetie," river float Karen said, and I guess there was nothing remotely racist about the comment because river float Karen *was* a progressive liberal, "but I said I am a teacher."

"What's that have to do with anything?" I asked river float Karen.

"I work *hard* for my three months of summer vacation, buster," she said, glaring at me while she said it. "I'm taking it!"

"We're never coming back to the south," beta-male said, but this time there was not even a sign of attempted bravado. He'd whispered it to river float Karen, but I'd heard it.

"Oh, five years from now, I'll be free, and I can go anywhere I want. We're leaving this whole damn country!" river float Karen said.

"Why don't you just leave now?" I said. "We'll help you pack. Are you on probation or something?"

"You listen," beta-male said, and he pointed at me, though he still made no eye contact.

"I'm listening?" I said, but beta-male had nothing further to say.

"I have five years to go until I get my pension," river float Karen said.

"Oh, yeah," I said. "The soul trap."

"The what?" river float Karen said.

"Pensions are part of the soul trap," I said. "Your sucked into a job you may or may not even like, but you refuse to leave once you've been there a few years, because you get free health insurance you never use and if you stick it out for thirty years, you will receive a pension, which pays you sixty percent of what you need to live on so that you only have to work part time for the rest of your life."

"We're done talking to you," river float Karen said, and she and beta-male began paddling backward with their arms to get further out into the river, where the current was much stronger, so they could float further down the river. To my surprise, I heard people clapping, and I turned and saw that we'd garnered an audience. My fellow dumb southerners along the river bank that day had been very pleased with the show I had given them.

I made my way to the lower portion of the Bigfoot Sasquatch hole and watched river float Karen and beta-male as they rounded the turn and made their way almost out of sight.

And that's when I saw it!

Finally!

Beta-male was drifting about twenty yards ahead of his wife. I guess that since he only weighed about half as much as his wife the current had carried him ahead, faster. Then Suddenly, something huge, which at first I thought was merely a boulder, shot quickly toward river float Karen. All of a sudden, what I'd thought was a boulder rose from the water. I knew the water in this part of the river was about five feet deep, yet the water came up only to this mighty creature's waist.

With one arm, it's right arm, the creature, which may or may not have been, potentially now, a Bigfoot Sasquatch reached out and grabbed river float Karen by the hair of her head. And even though river float Karen weighed every bit of two hundred pounds if she weighed an ounce, the creature lifted her off of her innertube (I think he, she, or it was merely showing off), and then slammed her into the water. It sunk back down into the water, giving the appearance of merely being a boulder again, and it held river float Karen under.

Forever!

She never came back up.

The End

(Postscript)

Whatever became of beta-male?

Who gives a fuck!

The Mysterious Case Of The Bigfoot Sasquatch Makeup Tutorial Girls

"I need your help, Dr. Drake," county sheriff's deputy Burt Reynolds said, approaching the area's local cryptozoologist, who was in his backyard reading a collection of short stories written by Ray Bradbury. "I sure hate to intrude on you unannounced like this, and I hope it's not a problem."

"As long as you don't mind coming up on another man in his drawers," Drake said. When the weather was nice, as it was on this mid-autumn afternoon, Drake preferred to read outside wearing only his boxers. There were no neighbors within sight of his yard, as he owned a sizable lot, and the lack of confinement by way of clothing had always allowed him to feel closer to nature and the universe as a whole.

"I had the damndest thing happen yesterday," Reynolds said, and he pulled a smartphone out of his pocket as he did. He looked down at it and said, "I listened to the whole story, and I know the girls aren't lying. It's their truth, as young women these days like to say. And I've gone over the evidence here on their phone, and it all checks out. But…" he trailed off, knowing not what to say next.

"And?" Drake said, dog-earing the page he was on and laying the book on the ground beside him. He was in his favorite vinyl camping/campfire/tailgating chair, and he had a can of

Ovaltine beside him. Oh, how he loved to drink Ovaltine when he read outside in his boxers.

"Well," Reynolds said. "I really hate to put you out. And I'm sure your wife doesn't want company."

"My wife's in the Philippines," Drake said. "Off to see her parents."

"You didn't go?" Reynolds said, the statement more a question.

"I left that place for a reason," Drake said, "and we'll leave it at that."

"If you don't mind then," Reynold said, tapping the password one of the girls, Kim, had given him into the iphone. "I'd like to have you take a look at this video." He handed the phone to Drake. "I'll give you a little backstory first, though."

"I'm all ears," Drake said, picking up his Ovaltine and taking a sip.

***

Deputy Burt Reynonds had been driving his cruiser down state route 601 the day before, a day as clear and beautiful as the day he would visit Drake for his professional opinion. The day had been uneventful, like most days as far as any crime went, and Reynolds had no complaints. One of the advantages to working in a high net worth area was that most of the crime, if there ever *was* any, was white collar in nature. The IRS saw more action on Burt's beat than any actual police officer.

Then, all of a sudden, Burt saw something completely unusual in the road about one hundred yards in front of him after coming around a sharp turn. Two girls, who looked like Chinese Geishas to him, jumping up and down in the middle of the road, trying to flag him down.

"Help us!" both girls were shouting, to Burt's surprise, in perfect English and with a southern accent. "It's coming!"

Burt turned on his flashers and stopped right in the middle of the road. He got out of his cruiser and both girls, about twenty years old, came running to him and threw their arms around him. "We have to get out of here," they said. They'd been crying and sweating, and the very hideously applied makeup on their faces had run and now appeared even more hideous. Burt couldn't help but notice that under their Geisha type robes, both girls were earring bikinis. Bikinis with the design of the American flag on them.

"Get in the back," Burt said, opening the back door of his cruiser. The girls were more than happy to oblige him and they jumped in. Burt quickly drew his service revolver and turned and faced toward the forest, holding his weapon up at eye level. "How tall is he?" he asked. He'd left his driver's door open so the girls had no problem hearing him.

"About eight feet," one of the girls, Kim said.

"More like ten," the other girl, Sue said. And she pronounced *ten* with two syllables, like "tee-in." Though she looked Asian, Burt thought, this girl has got to be from the south.

Burt realized he was being duped. He lowered his revolver and holstered it. He turned to face the girls in the backseat of his car. They were beautiful, despite the make-up issues they were having, and they were sexy as could be. And though they appeared to be purely Asian, their accents were more southern American than his, and he'd been born and raised in central Virginia. "Do you girls mind telling me what's going on here?" he said.

"Get us out of here first," Kim said, and Burt knew that whether he was being put on or not, Kim was scared, and so was Sue. Just because something might not be as it seems, or even true, people who are convinced that something is as it seems, or that something false is true, aren't lying when making their statements. These girls were not lying, Burt could tell. He knew they were scared and they didn't feel safe, so he got in his cruiser and took them downtown to hear their story, and oh, what a story they had to tell.

***

"We're screwed!" Kim told Sue, storming into their shared apartment on Jefferson Park Avenue in Charlottesville, Virginia. They'd been roommates the year before during their freshman year at UVA and they'd really hit it off well, so they decided to live together again, off campus, this year as sophomores.

"What's wrong?" Sue asked Kim, looking up from her smartphone. She had been watching the new Sam Hunt video on YouTube. Like Hunt, Sue, and ironically Kim as well, was from Georgia, and she absolutely loved country music, especially Sam Hunt's because she thought he was a hunk.

"We've been outed on Reddit," Kim said. "We've lost a thousand subscribers in the last hour.

"We're not *on* Reddit," Sue said.

"Our YouTube subscribers, you dumb hick!" Kim said.

"What!" Sue said, now sitting up quickly, dropping her i-phone to the floor, Sam Hunt immediately forgot.

"That little Japanese bitch, Himari, outed us on Reddit to steal our market share," Kim said, turning her phone around and showing Sue the post.

Their jig was up. Sue and Kim, both from Georgia, had built one hell of a following on YouTube by jointly hosting a channel called CuteKoreanGirlsMakeUpTutorials. Three times a week, for the past year, they would make videos where they dressed up like Geishas, wearing only bikinis under their robes which they always left untied and opened, and speaking in the cutest of Korean accents, and in broken English, of course, making them come across as more naive and innocent, and they would give tutorials on how to apply makeup Korean style.

The thing was, neither Kim nor Sue were Korean. They'd never even *been* to Korea. Both sets of their grandparents had migrated from Korea after the Korean war, escaping the North just before lockdown. Their grandparents, like many immigrants from other nations, clung strongly to the Korean community in Atlanta, where they'd set up shop after making the voyage to America. Kim and Sue's parents were products of that tightly knit second generation of Korean immigrants, and thus the girls' pure Korean ethnicities, but that's where it all stopped. Kim and Sue were raised in nice middle class suburban neighborhoods, and most of their friends were white, the second largest ethnicity represented among their childhood friends had been black, and they both only knew a handful of other Asians. The girls never knew each other before meeting at UVA, because they'd gone to different high schools in Atlanta, and the fact that they both came from Korean backgrounds was purely coincidental.

"Look at this shit," Sue said to Kim, pointing at one of the comments under Himari's post that outed them.

"If I wanted an American woman," the comment began," I'd get me one. I watch their YouTube show because I want an Asian woman! I've been duped. This is pure bait and switch!"

"I'm gonna kick Himari's ass when I see her," Kim said. "We helped her set up her channel and sent our subscribers to her so she could get monetized quicker, and now she's doing this? Stabbing us in the back just so she can take our audience?"

The girls continued reading the insults from their former fans, their base of which was diminishing by one thousand subscribers per hour now. The girls knew that their fans were not girls and women who wanted to know how to apply makeup in the traditional Korean way. They knew their fanbase was mostly a bunch of redneck white men, most of them older, who had a thing for young, petite, beautiful, sexy Asian women. They'd never had a problem with it, either. They were doing it purely for the Google Adsense revenues their videos generated, just like every other millennial who was making bank on social media. The girls often sat and talked with other social media content creators and they were all always wondering why they were even going to college in the first place. There was no way that the professions they'd pursue after graduation would provide as much income as many of them were already making on social media. Sue and Kim were both in education, and if they were to actually go into teaching after graduation they would take a massive pay cut.

"What are we gonna do?" Sue said.

"We're gonna kick Himari's ass," Kim said, again making her intentions for their little Japanese frenemy known.

"No we're not," Sue said.

"Why not?" Kim asked. "She wants the world to see who we really are? Let's get all redneck on her ass and give her a good, old fashioned southern beatdown!"

"That's exactly what she wants," Sue said, now feeling herself calming. "Then she could have one of those social media wars like those makeup dudes on YouTube. It would give her more power."

"So what do we do?" Kim asked.

"We switch gears," Sue said.

"How do you mean?" Kim said.

"Look," Sue said, now picking her i-phone up off the floor. "What a hunk he is," she said, seeing that Sam Hunt was still singing. She didn't listen to the rest of the song, though. She went to the homepage and scrolled down the recommended videos. "Look at all this shit," she said, holding the phone over for Kim to see.

"Bigfoot Sasquatch?" Kim said.

"Yeah," Sue said. "This shit is one of the most popular subjects on YouTube."

"What's that have to do with us?" Kim said.

"Who're our biggest fans?" Sue asked.

"Creepy old white guys," Kim said.

"Exactly!" Sue said. "And guess who makes up the biggest portion of the fanbase for Bigfoot Sasquatch?"

Kim's eyes widened, and a smile came to her face. "Creepy old white guys!" she said, excited.

"Exactly!" Sue said. "Get your boots, girl. We're going hiking."

***

"Can you believe that bullshit?" Kim said to Sue as she drove her Jeep Wrangler five over the speed limit through the city streets of Charlottesville, like most of the UVA students. The girls were heading to the outskirts of town. Ivy Creek Nature area. They'd done a Google search, and it was the closest place to their location that was off campus and had forested trails. They'd hiked through the trails on campus before and knew them to be too populated with people to be able to do what they needed to do. They needed to make it look like they were totally secluded and all alone. "There wasn't a damn thing in any of those videos, and all those people in the comments were putting time stamps where they saw shit, and there was nothing."

"I know," Sue said in agreement. "But you know, that one video. Where that guy was doing like a three sixty panoramic view of the leaves in the fall. That sure as shit looked like something huge on two legs walking down the hill. And it looked like it ducked behind a tree when he stopped panning the camera."

"You mean that one video from that dork that lives around here somewhere?" Kim said.

"Yeah."

"I'm sure he had his buddy in a monkey suit doing that," Kim said. "The timing was too perfect. There is *no way* he could capture something like that on film by tricking the creature into thinking he wasn't out there to actually capture it on film. I mean, who does that kind of shit? It had to be fake."

"Yeah," Sue said, thinking logically now. "You're right."

The girls may or may not have believed what they saw in the video of the guy discovering the lair of Bigfoot Sasquatch and being told he wasn't welcome, but they liked his strategy and they decided to adopt it. They were going to keep their YouTube channel named as it was, because they didn't want to go through the entire process of rebuilding a new one, but they were definitely going to make a pivot. Oh, they were still going to do the makeup tutorials, but they would now be doing them in the woods, claiming that they were trying to lure in the mysterious beast known as Bigfoot Sasquatch with their beauty and sexiness.

"Do you think this will actually work?" Sue asked Kim an hour later and after hiking for thirty minutes into the woods.

"Of course," Kim said. "What could creepy old white guys like more than smoking hot Asian chicks and Bigfoot Sasquatch?"

"Beer and Nascar?" Sue said.

"Oh ye of little faith," Kim said. She had been raised a southern baptist. "Let's do it here. Set the tripod up."

Sue did as she was told, and after a three, two, one, the camera was rolling, and Kim and Sue were confessing to their followers that they weren't really Korean. They were as American as baseball and apple pie. And they apologized to anyone who'd felt duped, but hey, they were still good to look at. They were still sweet and petite, and they would still do their makeup tutorials in their bikinis and Geisha robes, but there were going to be a few changes.

Another three, two, one and the girls lost their robes revealing a new style of bikinis. Old Glory! The red, white and blue!

"We're here to show you our true colors!" they said in unison. They'd practiced it on their hike out into the woods.

"Now," Kim said, peering into the camera at close range. "Here's something else we're going to be doing differently, too." Sue began looking all around them, really paranoid like, as if the two girls were being watched by some*one* or some*thing*. "We're going to attempt to use our beauty and our sexiness to lure in the mysterious creature known as Bigfoot Sasquatch," Kim said.

Kim drew away from the camera and Sue slowly, methodically, took her place. "We've heard it on good account that there have been several sightings in this area," Sue said as Kim was now looking around, all paranoid like, behind them. "Don't pay attention to what I'm doing," Sue said, pulling a tube of lipstick out of the pocket of her robe and beginning to apply it to her luscious lips. "Pay attention to what may or may not be behind me watching me put on my makeup." She was trying to do things just like that one weirdo who'd made the video about the lair.

The girls both applied their makeup in front of the camera, taking turns, of course, one doing makeup while the other acted all paranoid and crazy in the background. They made sure to take timed pauses and say, "did you hear that?" or "what was that?" every now and then to make it seem real, and they did their best to act scared a time or two.

"Do you really think this is going to work?" Kim asked Sue as she packed away the camera and tripod in her backpack when they were finished shooting the video.

"Where the fuck are we?" Sue said, as if she hadn't heard Kim's question.

"What do you mean?" Kim asked, looking around.

"When did we step off the trail?" Sue asked.

"Oh, fuck!" Kim said, realizing the trail was nowhere in sight. "Oh, fuck," she said again, as if saying it twice might help their situation.

"Follow me," Sue said. "We came from this direction."

"No we didn't," Kim said, refusing to move. "That's the way we were going. We came from the opposite direction."

"Shit!" Sue said, turning and following Kim. Though the girls were true southerners, they'd never spent much time in the woods. Much as in *any* away from the few times they'd hiked in the very well and populated trails on the campus of the University of Virginia. In a word, they were screwed, and they knew it.

"What was that?" Kim said a few minutes after they'd started their walk, not sure of where they were heading. She stopped upon having heard something and Sue had actually run into her back because she'd been following so closely.

"Come on," Sue said. "We're not recording anymore. Stop fucking around."

"I'm serious," said Kim. "It came from over there." She pointed her finger and Sue looked, and just as both girls thought they were staring at a giant stump from a fallen oak tree, what they'd thought was a stump stood, opened a large set of eyes, and let out a scream like nothing they'd ever heard before.

"Oh shit!" they both screamed, and then they turned and began running the opposite way. They ran and they ran, and they ran some more. They ran for a full ten minutes, grape vines and branches and briars whipping and scratching across their beautiful Korean looking but purely American faces.

"Oh, shit!" Sue yelled, stopping instantly in her tracks. "Another one!"

Kim looked twenty yards ahead and to the right, and sure enough, there, standing at least eight feet tall, if not taller, stood a creature that was only supposed to exist in urban legend and folklore. The girls took a quick turn to their left, about forty five degrees, and began running for their lives again.

"Are you getting this on camera?" Sue asked Kim.

"No," she yelled, and then she pulled out her i-phone and started recording. "But I will!"

Twice more during their time in the woods the girls were confronted by Bigfoot Sasquatch. Was it the same one? Were there multiple beasts among them? They did not know, but they dared not stop running, always changing their direction as dictated by the location of the beast or beasts, and with each new encounter, Kim captured at least fragments, blurry images at best, on her smartphone.

Finally, and at long last, the girls came to a road, old Virginia state route 601. And they came to the road just in time. A car was coming around the bend. They began jumping up and down, their Geisha gowns flowing in the light breeze created by their jumping. And as their good fortune would have it, the car that was pulling up to them, slowing as it came, turned out to be a police car. Its flashers were on, and it came to a stop and a not too unattractive man just old enough to be the girls' father stepped out of the car and came to their rescue.

***

"So what do you make of this?" Burt Reynolds asked local cryptozoologist Dr. Drake as Drake handed the deputy the girl's phone. He'd viewed the footage the girl was able to capture while running for what she thought was her life.

"Same thing you think but will never say in words," Drake said.

"So you're telling me," Reynolds said, "that this place is infested with Bigfoot Sasquatches."

"I don't know if I'd use the word *infested*," Drake said. "But there's a few."

"So what am I supposed to do?" Reynolds asked. "Ask the sheriff to ask the mayor to ask the Governor to call out the national guard? Track these things down and kill them?"

"Now why in the hell would you go and do a fool thing like that?" Drake asked in his Appalachian American accent. An accent that his former neighbor, Jittery Jay, used to mock, until, of course, Jittery Jay had had his unfortunate demise (see Bigfoot Sasquatch Files Volume 1).

"Well, it's clear these girls were running for their lives. These creatures, which may or may not be what they actually saw, were trying to kill them."

"Oh, my God," Drake said, rolling his eyes and putting a hand over his face. "Did you even watch the video?"

"Of course, I watched the video," Burt Reynolds said. "What am I missing."

"Obviously all of it," Drake said, removing his hand from his face and looking the sheriff's deputy square in the eyes.

"Enlighten me," Reynolds said.

"It was clear the girls were lost," Drake said. "The Bigfoot Sasquatch were helping them find their way out of the woods."

"What?" Reynolds said, incredulous.

"Watch it again if you need to," Drake said. "Every time the creatures showed up, it was to redirect the girls' direction of travel. The creatures could tell they were lost and needed to be shown the way out of the woods, so that's what they did. In a very nontraditional way, if you will."

"Hm," Reynolds said, and he pondered Drake's point. It made sense. It wasn't like these creatures, if that was indeed what they'd been, could just walk up to the girls and say, "hey, I can tell you're lost. Let me show you the way." The creatures know, for sure, that humans feared them, so the best they could do was scare the girls into heading in the right direction. "So what am I supposed to do about this, then?"

"What do you mean?" Drake asked, lost.

"You know," Reynolds said. "Just in the past couple of years we've had all these supposed bear attacks. That Jittery Jay guy and his wife. Crazy A (See Bigfoot Sasquatch Files Volume 3). And that Torrie woman. And her parents a few years before that (See Bigfoot Sasquatch Files Volume 2)."

"Weren't all those people assholes?" Drake asked.

"That's really no way to speak of the dead," Reynods said, "but yeah. Privilved snobs are what I'd call 'em."

"Then fuck 'em," Drake said. He took a sip of his Ovaltine and picked his book back up off the ground and began reading, dismissing the sheriff's deputy, in a word.

"So I should do nothing," Reynolds said. He didn't like being so nonchalantly dismissed.

"Maybe people shouldn't be assholes," Drake said. "Obviously those little Asian girls were okay. They made it out of their encounter without harm."

"So you're saying these things only kill assholes," Reynolds said.

"They are empaths," Drake said, and after that Reynolds simply turned and walked away. He went to see the girls at their apartment and convinced them that what they'd seen had not been what they'd thought they'd seen. "You were in a panic," he told them. "Your mind plays tricks on you when you're in a panic."

The girls bought it, hook line and sinker, and they said fuck social media and studied hard, and got their teaching degrees and went on to mold young minds and take a massive paycut…

And they never went into the woods again!

The End

Publish Or Perish

Professor Parish sat at the campfire with his six trusted students. These were the half dozen who'd made it through his trial by fire. Forty six students had begun the experiment, but only these six remained. He did his best to keep his eyes from favoring Marta, his favorite of these six elite, but it was difficult, because he was only human, and a very healthy *male* human, at that, and Marta *was* drop dead gorgeous. Twenty two, half black on her father's side, and half Thai on her mother's- Blasian, as the cool kids said- and she was one hundred percent gorgeous, Dr. Parish thought!

"So when does the first test begin?" Marta asked, as the group sat in a circle around the stoned blaze.

"Any time now," Dr. Parish said. "Though most likely, it will happen after dark."

"Why's that?" Ricky asked. Dr. Parish hated Ricky, because he had good reason to believe Marta was crushing on Ricky. Ricky *was* good looking, and he *was* pretty intelligent, but, well, Dr. Parish was hoping Marta might crush on him. Unfortunately, the girl showed no signs of daddy issues, so at nearly fifty years old, Dr. Parish would simply have to accept living with fantasies when it came to all things Marta. But he'd decided he'd still hate Ricky, anyway, just for the sake of things.

"I think you'll understand when the time comes," Dr. Parish said. Had Marta asked the question, he would have rambled on for half an hour or so, trying to impress her with big words and such, but Ricky, well, reference the last paragraph.

"I've never been camping before," Alice said. Alice was okay, for a freshman. Actually highly intelligent, and pretty mature, but she had a tendency to talk too much about stuff no one cared about. Dr. Parish didn't respond to her comment, but someone else did. Sarah, perhaps. Dr. Parish wasn't paying attention. He was reminiscing in his mind. Not just about the social experiment he was carrying out, or the fame that would certainly come his way once he published his results, or the tenure that the University would no doubt grant him because of it, or of getting into Marta's pants, but about what happened at this very campsite with Dr. Parish and his childhood best friend- a man who'd been killed in Afghanistan during the war about a decade before- and of how he knew he was going back on the promise he'd made with his now deceased friend.

And of how he did *not* care!

***

Once upon a time, Dr. Parish was simply known as Billy. And his best friend, before being known as Army Sergeant First Class Byron Jones, was simply known as Byron. And Billy and Byron spent every waking hour of their youth together, either on the river banks catching trout, or in the woods hunting deer and turkeys. Many of their adventures were had during overnight or weekend camping trips, here, at Byron's grandfather's place- a small homestead a couple miles outside the city limits of their small, Appalachian town. The property wasn't big enough to be considered a farm, and the old man never raised any livestock. He had a couple garden spots is all. But it was secluded- out in the middle of nowhere, and when the sun went down it was as dark as a coal miner's asshole, unless the moon was full, at which time you could almost see as if it were daytime, and it was peaceful and pleasant, and it held the best memories of their youth.

And it was haunted.

Or something.

But it definitely had a Bigfoot Sasquatch living on it, because that one fall, back in October of 1987, Billy and Byron saw it!

Or her.

Or him.

Or they (because it may or may not have been alone).

And neither of them had ever forgotten.

And that had only been the first time they'd seen it. The creature, or creatures, obviously felt safe in the boys' presence, and out of curiosity, when the boys would stay at Byron's grandfather's place, out in the middle of nowhere, they would often come right up to them while the boys were sitting around the campfire at night. Sure, they'd keep their distance, so everyone involved would feel safe, but the boys could always make out their eyeshine and the outlines of their bodies. The boys never felt threatened in their presence, and they knew they had something special, and they'd made a pact, somewhere around 1990- senior year- that no matter what, neither of them would ever disclose the fact that there was potentially a small clan of Bigfoot Sasquatch living on Byron's grandfather's land. And they'd cut their hands and became blood brothers on a handshake to seal the deal!

***

But Byron got obliterated by a roadside bomb just outside of Kandahar in 2009.

And Billy's wife left him for a woman in 2012.

And the University refused to grant him tenure because of his 'extracurricular activities' with beautiful young coeds (oh, if only he could get Marta to join that list!).

So Billy was reneging on his pact with Byron, and to hell with the safety of those Bigfoot Sasquatches. Whatever came to them after the disclosure of their existence and location was no concern to Billy. He needed the tenure, he needed the security, and he wanted Marta, and if he didn't publish something of substance, soon, he knew he would perish, professionally and then personally. Dr. Parish had to do something that had never been done before, and document it, or Dr. Parish would become Dr. Perished.

***

Dr. Parish had begun his social experiment at the beginning of the semester, the fall semester, and how fitting that here the finalists were, sitting around the campfire at Byron's grandad's place in October, the very month of the first encounter Billy and Byron had had with the creatures all those years ago.

The first test was simple. All forty six volunteers stood in a circle. Dr. Parish whispered in the first participant's ear, "my wife left me for a woman." The thing of it all was that that volunteer then had to whisper the exact same thing into the ear of the volunteer beside them. And so it went around the circle until they came to the end, and then the final volunteer loudly proclaimed the secret that had been passed around.

The first trial saw half the students eliminated. "Your brother slept with your mother?" The final student both asked and proclaimed at the end of it. Dr. Parish then *walked back the cat*, as they call it in the C.I.A. (you did *not* read that here), a process by which you go backward with your information seeking. The final student who stated the wrong information was not kicked out of the study, because the student just in front of them admitted that that was exactly what he'd told her. The difficulty lied in finding the broken links of the chain. Who flubbed it up? Several trials had to be done, and Dr. Parish's wife leaving him for a woman was retold as his father was really his brother, and his uncle was gay, and in one trial, that his mother knew why the sky was blue, all before the trial was over and successful.

Dr. Parish was convinced some of the students were flubbing things up on purpose, just because they were being assholes, but he did point out with each trial that this was a prime example of how rumors get started and spread, and why you should believe very little of what you hear when it comes to gossip. "Don't believe anything you hear," Dr. Parish told his student volunteers, "and only half of what you see."

But he'd finally narrowed the field down to a dozen. And then came the next set of trials. Witness account trials.

Dr. Parish would have all one dozen of his students observe an act, such as a dog walking through the park, unleashed, and then urinating on a tree or a trash can, and then trotting back to its human to be leashed. He would then have the students write exactly what had happened, in the fewest amount of words as possible, and once again, he was *not* amazed to find how many of these students, literally half, had difficulty in either remembering and notating things exactly as they'd happened, or at least being able to put the events that had occurred in properly worded fashion. One student had the dog urinating on a tree, when it had clearly urinated on a trashcan. One student said the dog was big and black, when it was clearly small and brown.

With the final six student volunteers expelled from the study, Dr. Parish finally had the six that he needed. These six were good at repeating stories exactly as they'd heard them, and they were good at writing stories about events exactly as they had occurred. In a word, they were credible.

***

"What was that?" Marta asked, turning to look behind her. Darkness had fallen now, and she couldn't see a thing that was any further than a foot behind her. She'd been staring into the light of the fire, hence, she was blinded for the darkness.

"I heard it, too," Ricky said. Dr. Parish didn't know if Ricky had actually heard anything or if he was just supporting Marta. *Goddamn you, Ricky*, Dr. Parish thought to himself. *Don't fuck this up over a peace of ass. I need this.*

Just as Marta turned around to face the fire again a sound came from the woods behind her that everyone in the group heard. They all turned to look, and there, about ten feet away, stood a being that had to be at least ten feet tall. Everyone present could see the shining of its eyes as the fire reflected off of them.

"Oh, my God," Alice said.

"Everyone's okay," Dr. Parish said. "There's no need to panic. If you'd feel more comfortable coming over here and sitting on this side of the fire, so your back isn't to it, feel free. Just move slowly so that you don't scare it away. I can assure you it is not going to hurt any of us."

"How can you be so sure?" Alice asked.

"Because I've been coming here and seeing these creatures for longer than you guys have been alive," Dr. Parish said.

The students sitting on the opposite side of the fire as Dr. Parish took him up on his recommendation and joined him and the others on their side of the fire. They sat in silence, staring at the hulking dark figure that was not supposed to be real. Five minutes later, another creature, this one about seven feet tall stepped out of the darkness and joined it.

"I've never seen two together," Dr. Parish said. "They must be really curious about you guys."

A minute later, another came out, this one about five feet tall.

"I think they're a family," Marta said.

"I'll be," Dr. Parish said. He was completely amazed.

The family of Bigfoot Sasquatch stared at the campers as the campers stared back for about ten more minutes, and then, just as mysteriously as they'd shown up, they slipped back into the cover of darkness and were gone.

***

Thirty days later, Dr. Parish was a worldwide celebrity. He'd published his piece on the existence of Bigfoot Sasquatch, and not only had he been given tenure by the University, but he'd already earned more money being paid for speaking engagements on the weekends than he would earn all year from his professorship. Sadly, he'd not gotten anywhere with Marta, but that was okay, because he knew in time that that might change. At least he hoped so.

And now, on a crisp, cool Saturday morning just before Thanksgiving, he was preparing to earn $100,000.00 from a speaking engagement which he'd hyped up by publicizing that he would now reveal the location of the Bigfoot Sasquatch family that he and his credible, trusted student aids had observed.

And Marta was pissed!

None of the other students cared much about the success that Dr. Parish was having as a result of his publication. They were happy for him, at most, but beyond that, they had other things to do, like go tailgating at the University's football games, and partying balls all night after the games, win or lose. And partying balls on the nights when there were no games to win or lose.

But Marta? Well, she was different.

Marta was an empath, and she could feel much more than even a Ph. D. in sociology, like Dr. Parish, could imagine, because, she knew, the higher one's education, the less likely one is to believe in things such as empaths.

Marta had known from the day she met him that Dr. Parish had dirty thoughts about her. She could tell he was a self-centered narcissist, not unlike many of the professors she'd known during her college years, and she could tell he was self-seeking. Still, she thought he was okay, and she'd jumped at the chance to be in his experiment, because binge drinking around campus was not her thing, and her gut instinct had told her during the entire experiment that the man was doing something for personal gain.

Marta made sure to be in attendance today with the thousands of others in attendance at the University's baseball stadium (there was a home football game today, or they would have used the football stadium in order to sell more tickets), as well as the millions and millions of people at home watching the livestream feeds.

"Today," Dr. Parish stated, after rambling about how important he was for about ten minutes, "I will disclose to the world, the very location of the small family of Bigfoot Sasquatches my trusted students and I observed, and the world of science and curiosity seekers alike can descend upon the location and the world can now see for themselves!"

The crowd cheered at that. So many people already had their car keys in hand, ready to go to this mysterious location so they could see a Bigfoot Sasquatch for themselves.

"The exact location of these creatures," Dr. Parish said, and then he took a dramatic pause in order to bask in the glory of such a large crowd's utter silence.

"He's lying!" a beautiful dark skinned girl with long black hair shouted from the middle of the crowd. "I was there. I was one of his aides. It was all a hoax for his fame and fortune, and it's gone on long enough!"

The crowd gasped, making it sound as if the air had just been released from the tiny tight nozzles of ten thousand car tires all at once.

Dr. Parish was floored. He knew not what to say. He stared out at Marta, now realizing that any fantasies he had that involved her would never be fulfilled.

"He never promised us money," Marta said, continuing after the crowd ceased gasping. "He didn't bribe us. We did it all on our own accord, because like him, we wanted to see how gullible the masses were." At this, the crowd began murmuring. They, the masses, were offended. "It was all a social experiment," Marta said. "This was all just one big social experiment, and you've all been duped. There is no such thing as Bigfoot Sasquatch." And with that, Marta simply walked away, first down the aisle where she'd been seated, and then, out the front gates of the stadium. As soon as she exited the stadium, everyone in attendance stood up and did the same.

"Wait!" Dr. Parish shouted. "She's lying!"

No one listened to him, because no one cared. They knew they'd been duped. They were all the butt of his big joke. They all knew that there is no such thing as Bigfoot Sasquatch.

Dr. Parish lost his tenure. He was not paid for the day's event. He was fired from the University, and he could not find new employment in academia, because his career was done.

In a word, Dr. Parish had become…

… Dr. Perished.

The End

6

Ask Me No Questions I'll Tell You No Lies

"So, I'm not trying to pry or anything," Jacob Mack said to his new hire, Jimmy Blake, as they trucked down the beautiful Virginia biway outside of Charlottesville. Jacob was driving the commercial sized dump truck, loaded to the gills with giant white oak and red oak logs that his tree removal service company had just cleared from the yard of a wealthy Virginia landowner. There were many wealthy Virginia landowners in this part of the state. Most of them were trust babies and Virginia first families, families whose ancestors had been awarded huge land grants by King James himself shortly after the settlement of Jamestown. Whereas most people in most other places would cut up any fallen timber themselves, and use said timber for firewood, most of the folks in this area were more than happy to pay Mack's Tree Removal Services up to five thousand dollars for each tree for cutting them up and hauling them away. The residents did not view their fallen trees as free firewood, rather, they viewed them as eyesores. Though most of their homes had multiple fireplaces, they burned gas in them so as to eliminate any labor, and most of them, sadly, simply covered their fireplaces up with large, flatscreen televisions. "But when you lost your CDL for drinking and driving, was that the first time you'd gone to work drinking like that?," Mack continued, prodding, "Or was it the first time you'd gotten caught?"

"Ask me no questions, I'll tell you no lies," Jimmy said. Jimmy was in his early thirties and had been only a handful of years away from actually retiring from a major delivery company. He'd started with the company at seventeen years old, driving forklifts in the warehouse, and he'd gotten his CDL at twenty and began hauling shipments by way of tractor trailers. Unfortunately, Jimmy had a drinking problem, and once he'd been switched to driving nights, he took his problem with him to work most nights, as well as a cooler with an iced down twelve pack of beer in it.

"But you're straight now," Mack said.

"Been sober just over a year," Jimmy said. "And I really do appreciate you giving me a second chance by hiring me. My old employer wouldn't even reply to my calls or emails, and a lot of former friends and family members have written me off as a deadbeat forever."

"Those who matter don't mind when we make mistakes, and we all do, and those that mind don't matter," Mack said.

"What?" Jimmy said, turning to face the older man. Mack was about sixty. Jimmy had been watching the scenery blow by. Though he was from Virginia, he wasn't from this part of Virginia, and he'd never been through this area. He found it to be absolutely beautiful, but he had to admit, his mouth had begun watering a bit a mile or so back when they'd passed Bigfoot Sasquatch Brewing Company, a microbrewery out here in the middle of nowhere, surrounded by nothing but natural scenic beauty and beautiful, vast estates.

"What it means is," Mack said, "that anyone who isn't your friend anymore because you got busted for doing something that most people have done at one point or another, they just never got caught, then they weren't your real friends in the first place."

"Yeah," Jimmy said, thinking about it for a minute. Mack had a point, he believed.

"And as far as family goes?" Mack said. "How many of those fuckers would you have had anything to do with, anyway, if you hadn't been kin?"

Jimmy again thought Mack had a pretty good point. He had a couple of sisters who he could never stand who always wanted to just through any mistake he'd ever made in his face. Last Thanksgiving, the last time he'd seen them, they were all about asking him how it felt to have been six years away from a pension at such a young age and then fucking it all up. "You're pretty wise," Jimmy said to Mack.

"I've been around the block, kid," Mack said. "And half the guys working for me fucked up at some point. You ain't the only one on my payroll with a D.U.I. on record. And them other guys- and I ain't gonna tell ya who they are, cause that's *their* business- well, they've turned out to be some of the best workers I've ever had."

Both men stared ahead. They were getting close to their destination; 'ol Leroy's, as Mack and his employees referred to the place. It was a huge farm, though no farming was done there. The man that owned the place was named Leroy Jenkins. A long time friend of Jacob Mack's.

"Looky, here," Mack said, pointing to a tractor trailer loaded down with split and stacked firewood coming out of the dirt road that was Leroy Jenkins' driveway. "'Ol Leroy sells more firewood, commercially, than anyone in central Virginia. That load there's probably going down to the Carolinas."

After the truck hauling the split and stacked firewood had cleared the turn, Jacob Mack turned his huge dump truck into Jenkins' drive. "I'll come out here with you the first couple times, for your training and all," Mack said. "Show you where to put the stuff. Introduce you to 'ol Leroy. But I'd say you'll be on your own by the end of the week."

Though Jimmy had lost his CDL license due to his D.U.I. the previous year, he could still drive a dump truck. The state of Virginia did not require a CDL for such purposes, just a driver's license, which Jimmy had just gotten back after having had it suspended for a year, and proper dump truck driver's training, which he was getting on the job now, at the hands of his new boss, Jacob Mack.

"There he sits, now," Mack said, slowing down as he pulled up to a somewhat dilapidated old farm house. There was a man of about seventy years old sitting on the front porch. He looked half asleep and half dead to Jimmy, but just as Jimmy started to think he really may be one or the other, the man stood, and with the use of a four legged walker, he made his way over to the big truck.

"Afternoon, 'ol buddy," Jenkins said to Mack when he got close enough to be heard over the truck's engine.

"Say there, partner," Mack said back. "Meet my new man, here. Name's Jimmy Blake. He'll be hauling this stuff out here by himself by next week, I'm sure."

Jenkins, very slowly, made his way around to the other side of the truck. Once there, he reached up toward the window and shook hands with Jimmy, who'd leaned out the window and reached down.

"You'll have to excuse me," Jenkins said. "I's out splittin' and stacking firewood this morning, and my back's a little sore. That's why I'mma usin' this here walker and gettin' around a little slower than usual."

"It's okay," Jimmy said. "It's a pleasure to meet you, Sir."

"They'll be none of that Sir nonsense around here," Jenkins said with a light laugh. "My dad was Sir, and he was the meanest son of a bitch I ever knew. You just call me 'ol Leroy, like everyone else."

"Will do," Jimmy said, and at that Mack pulled the dump truck forward.

The road that was Jenkins' driveway continued past the old house and headed into the woods. After about half a mile's drive of pure forest, things opened up again, revealing a large field about twenty acres in size and it was filled with firewood. Half split and stacked, and the other still in humongous log form. Another tractor trailer was just leaving the field having picked up a full load of split and stacked firewood. It was on it's way to Georgia.

"Damn," Jimmy said in awe. 'Ol Leroy's firewood operation was larger than most lumber mills Jimmy had ever seen.

"We ain't the only one that brings him wood," Mack said. "See, if we hauled this here load we have now to a landfill, they'd charge us seventy five dollars to dump it. 'Ol Leroy lets us bring it here for free, and, well, you can see what he does with it. He turns it into one hundred percent profit. I don't care that he makes a small fortune off of what we give him for free, because he saves us three hundred dollars a day. Do the math on that. Comes out to over seventy thousand dollars a year. That's profit of mine I get to keep in my bank and use to pay my men. I'm happy to give him all this wood for free."

"How long's he been doing this?" Jimmy asked, looking around, still amazed.

"About twenty years," Mack said.

"Where's all his workers?" Jimmy asked, realizing now that since the other trucker had left, he and Jacob Mack were the only two people to be seen. Mack didn't answer. He actually acted like he hadn't heard the question. "Where's his equipment?" Jimmy then asked, realizing there were no woodmizers or firewood belt operated cutting machines. An operation of this size, Jimmy assumed, would require the most state of the art commercial grade firewood cutting equipment money could buy. Again, Mack didn't answer.

"This is our area," Mack said when he finally did speak again. "Jump out and guide me back, and lets dump this load up as tight against the last load we brought as we can, so we can fit as much in here as we can in the future. That's the key. Pack it in tight in case it takes him a while to get around to it."

Jimmy hopped down from the truck and guided Jacob Mack back. Jacob Mack dumped their load and Jimmy jumped back in the truck and the two men began heading back to the home where they'd been working, expecting their crew to have another large oak that had fallen in a recent storm ready for loading.

Jimmy looked all around as they drove out of the massive log yard, and what he did see in the way of firewood splitting equipment was axes. Dozens of them. All scattered around, stuck into variously placed splitting blocks. It looked as if a couple dozen people had been out in the log yard splitting these massive logs with splitting axes.

"What's going on here?" Jimmy said, looking over as Mack as they entered the wooded portion of the drive before reaching Jenkins' house.

"Word is," Mack said, "'Ol Leroy splits and stacks all this wood himself."

"What?" Jimmy said. "At his age? With that back? And enough to supply the eastern seaboard with firewood?"

Mack did not reply.

"What's really going on here?" Jimmy asked.

"Ask me no questions, I'll tell you no lies," Mack said, and he looked over at Jimmy and gave him a wink that said *if you aren't willing to talk to me about certain truths, I'm not willing to talk to you about certain truths.*

As they drove past 'ol Leroy's house, Jimmy looked over and noticed that 'ol Leroy was enjoying his afternoon nap in a hammock he had set up in his yard over on the side of his house opposite the driveway. He was so fast asleep, Jimmy could hear him snoring over the loud engine of the dump truck he was in. Well, Jimmy thought, at least he isn't dead.

***

Jimmy finished up his first week, his training week, and just as Mack had told him, he was now driving on his own. During his first week solo, he'd gone to 'ol Leroy's three times, but all three times, 'ol Leroy had been nowhere to be seen. Jimmy put the large logs where he'd been instructed to put them during his training week, and each of the three times he'd taken loads out, he saw that the load previously taken before each had already been sawed down, split and stacked. There was no way, Jimmy thought, that a seventy year old man who could barely hobble around in his yard, with the use of a walker at that, could cut, split and stack so much wood in such a short period of time. Especially without industrial equipment. Something was going on here, Jimmy knew, and he was determined to figure out what it was.

***

"Maybe he's breaking child labor laws," Jimmy said to himself the following week while driving his first load of logs out to 'ol Leroys' place. These logs were maple. Still an excellent wood for burning. "Or prisoners," Jimmy said. "I bet he's buddies with the warden over at the county jail, and he buses some of the prisoners in here at night and makes 'em chop all that wood with axes. Hard labor."

Jimmy reached 'ol Leroy's drive and waited patiently as not one, nor two, but three tractor trailers filled with split and stacked firewood pulled out of the drive. Once the coast was clear, he turned into the drive, and he was happy to see 'ol Leroy standing in the front yard, propping himself up on his walker.

"Afternoon, 'ol Leroy," Jimmy said, sticking his head out the window.

"How's things going, 'ol buddy?" Leroy said, hobbling over toward the truck.

"Good," Jimmy said. "Real good. Hey," Jimmy said, excitedly, thinking quick on his feet, "it's about my lunch break. I packed a lunch, but how about after I dump this load I come back around here and sit with you for a spell while I eat, so we can get to know each other a little better."

"Sounds good to me, 'ol buddy," Leroy said. "I'll be a sittin' there on the porch. If I doze off, why, just wake me up. Not too sudden though," he said. "I was in Nam, and I might come to and knock ya a good one upside the head."

"All right," Jimmy said, laughing lightly. "We wouldn't want that." And with that, he began moving forward again. He made his way through the forested part of Leroy's property and then was in the twenty acre field that was the largest commercial firewood operation he'd ever seen. Again, he took note of how he saw no employees today, just like he'd never seen any employees ever. Still, no commercial equipment. Just dozens of splitting axes stuck into dozens of chopping blocks sporadically placed around the field.

***

"Glad you're awake," Jimmy said, carrying his small cooler onto Leroy's porch. It was actually the cooler he used to use to keep his beer cold while driving for his former employer, but these days it only held food. "I was hoping I wouldn't have to wake you. I sure do enjoy my naps when I can get 'em."

"I'll just take mine after you leave," Leroy said. "So how's the new job workin' out for ya?"

"Going good," Jimmy said. "Real good." He sat down and pulled a roast beef and provolone cheese sandwich with mustard on a hamburger bun out of his cooler. He took the sandwich out of the ziplock back it was in and ate almost half of it with the first bite.

"You're hungry," 'ol Leroy said.

"I don't eat breakfast," Jimmy said.

"Gotta eat," Leroy said. "If you're gonna work, you need the calories."

"I bet you eat like a buffalo," Jimmy said, just before putting almost the entirety of the remainder of his sandwich in his mouth. Alas, it would take him three bits to devour this one.

"Ha, ha, ha," Leroy laughed, but he spoke no real words.

"I mean, with all the wood splittin' you do," Jimmy said, talking with his mouth full. "How on earth do you do all that by yourself?"

"Well," 'ol Leroy said. "I get a little help."

"From who?" Jimmy said. "Must be more than a little. You couldn't split and stack as much firewood as you do as quickly as you do if you had the best machinery you could get. And you don't have *any* machinery." Jimmy swallowed the food in his mouth then stuck the small bit of sandwich that remained into his mouth. "And what's up with all the axes? There is *no way* all that wood's gettin' split up by some of your buddies using axes."

"Why don't you come on out tonight and help me and my buddies," 'ol Leroy said. "If you really want to know."

"Tonight?" Jimmy said, looking up. He'd been digging through his cooler for his next sandwich. "Your helpers come out and do all this work at night?"

"Yeah," Leroy said.

"But I didn't even see any lights out there," Jimmy said.

"They don't need 'em," Leroy said.

"Why not?" Jimmy said, now taking the sandwich he'd dug out of the cooler out of its ziplock bag.

"Because they can see in the dark," Leroy said.

Jimmy had just bitten into his sandwich, and with Leroy's last comment, he'd stopped moving entirely. He looked like the frozen statue of The Thinker, but with a sandwich in his mouth.

Leroy stood and turned toward the door of his house. "I think I'll be takin' me that nap now," he said. "Stay and eat all your lunch. And if you wanna see how the most amazing firewood operation the world over operates, show up about ten o'clock." And with that, he went inside to have his nap.

Jimmy ate the bite of sandwich that was in his mouth, but he put the rest of his sandwich in his cooler and stood and began making his way back to Jacob Mack's dump truck. Curiosity had just killed his appetite.

***

Jimmy pulled his personally owned vehicle, an old Jeep Wrangler, into 'ol Leroy's driveway as darkness fell, about seven p.m., as it was now mid-October in Virginia. He got out and began walking up the porch steps before looking up and noticing that 'ol Leroy was sitting on the porch in the same chair he always seemed to be sitting in.

"You're early," 'ol Leroy said. He was drinking a cup of coffee. He offered Jimmy a cup, but Jimmy declined, claiming he'd never sleep if he drank coffee this late.

"I live an hour south of Charlottesville," Jimmy said. "I don't think I could wait until ten to come out and then make it home by a decent time and then get up for work tomorrow. I hope you don't mind me coming out early."

"Not at all," Leroy said. "But the action ain't gonna start for a few more hours."

"Look," Jimmy said, sitting on the top porch step. "I don't have to see it. You seem like a pretty straight shooter. I'd like to just hear what's going on out here, from your mouth, to settle my curiosity, I guess. I'll take you at your word, and then I'll get home before it's too late so I can get some sleep."

"Well," 'ol Leroy said. "I can tell you exactly how it all happened, but I'm tellin' ya now, you ain't gonna believe a word of it, and you'll be convinced I'm crazier than a shithouse rat."

"Try me," Jimmy said.

"All right," Leroy said. He took a sip of coffee, and then he began telling his story, and it went like this.

***

Thirty years before, Leroy Jenkins had been a mail carrier. He'd lost his job because everyday, after getting his route done early, he'd stop by one of the local pubs to have a few beers and milk out the clock for the rest of the day. He would joke about it when he got back to the post office, half lit or more than half lit, about how he was getting paid to drink beer.

Until the day he drove his mail truck into the ass end of a school bus.

The bus was stopped, and the last child had just gotten off. No one was injured. Not a single scratch. But the police came, of course, to file a report, and they noticed that Jenkins had been drinking. He failed their field sobriety test, was given a D.U.I. and summarily lost his job as a mailman.

Jenkins knew a guy who knew a guy who knew a guy who had just started up a tree removal service company and who was looking for help. Jenkins met up with the guy, Jacob Mack, and was not only given a second chance at employment, but would find a good, true friend in Mack, in time. Mack, too, benefited professionally, because as it turned out, Jenkins had been left his family's farm just a few years before when his mother had died. Mack was making money hand over fist removing fallen trees for all the rich people in the area, but a considerable portion of his profits were being handed out by having to pay landfills and private landowners to dump the removed trees on their properties. When Jenkins first heard of this, he told Mack that that was poppycock, and that he had a twenty acre field out in the middle of the woods about a half mile behind his old farmhouse, and that Mack could put as many trees as he wanted back there for free.

"I'm gonna tell ya now, though," Jenkins had said. "I'm probably gonna cut and split it up and sell it as firewood. So I'll be making something off of it."

"So what," Mack had told him in reply. "You'll be saving me a small fortune. I don't care what you do with it."

And with that, their deal had been struck.

Jenkins' family's farm had been in the family since the mid 1800's, and during that entire period, the family had never allowed anyone to hunt on the land. Sure, they took the occasional deer and a bunch of squirrels and rabbits at times, especially when times were tough, which they occasionally were, but no one else had ever been granted that permission. The story as to why this was, a story passed down from generation to generation, was that it was because there were certain forest creatures living on the property that the family felt needed to be protected. The family had learned that in protecting these creatures, these creatures would protect them in return.

How?

Well, there were several occasions back in the late 1920's and early 1930's, during the depression, when times had been really tough. Even wild game was hard to come by, because so many people were out there hunting, killing everything that moved, because if they didn't, they would have no meat to eat. The American wild turkey nearly became extinct during this period, and all because so many people were so hungry.

The Jenkins family fared well during that period, because, once a week, and for a number of years, they would open their front door of an early morning, and there, hanging in an old hickory nut tree in the front yard, by wild grapevine, would be a whitetail deer, only recently killed. The family would have meat for the entire week. And the following week? Like clockwork, they'd have fresh vinision hanging in their old hickory nut tree again.

And then there was that time in the 1950's ('ol Leroy had been a boy and could remember this time well), when the house caught on fire in the middle of the night. It had been during the last harvest of the year. It was the first night of the year that the family was actually burning wood in their woodstove, and there had been a bird's nest built in the top of the flu earlier in the year that had caught fire. The cinders scattered across the roof and set the top portion of the eastward facing side of the house on fire. Everyone inside was exhausted from having worked the harvest all day and they did not wake up.

Until the banging on the outside of the house started! Just outside the downstairs bedroom windows.

The family rose and escaped the blaze. They fell back, fifty yards from the house to watch it burn, as they huddled together in blankets they'd brought with them from their beds, doing their best to stay warm in the chill night's air.

Their saviors' favors had not stopped with waking them. The family watched as tall, dark figures moving frantically in the night carried bucket after bucket of water from the pond in the backyard to the blaze and extinguished the flames, allowing them to have caused only minor damage.

But the most amazing part, at least as far as what Jimmy was here for tonight, was when they'd come to 'ol Leroy's aid when his back started going out and he was no longer able to do the backbreaking work that he'd been doing for about ten years for his new, best good buddy Jacob Mack.

True to his word, 'ol Leroy began cutting, splitting and stacking quite a bit of the wood that his buddy Jacob Mack was delivering to his giant field at the back of his farm. But 'ol Leroy was no spring chicken. He was beginning to get up there in years, and there had been a time or two when he'd lifted with his back instead of his legs. When he'd twisted this way when he should have twisted that way. And he didn't even like to *think* about what his body had been put through back in the war. The amount of work he was able to do was becoming greatly limited, and he knew that Jacob Mack could tell, and he had the feeling that the only reason his buddy was keeping him on at the job was because he didn't want to fire him because he was a friend. And he also knew that as his injuries progressed, he would be hard pressed to feed himself in his old age.

So he came up with a plan.

Jacob went through his out buildings and collected all the axes and splitting mauls and wedges and sledgehammers that he had. He put them in the back of his old Ford F250 and hauled them out to the field where Jacob had given him so much free firewood. He set up splitting stations throughout, and he went around, throughout the day, splitting and stacking wood at the various stations. The entire time he could feel eyes upon him, and knew that the entire time there were eyes upon him.

At the end of the day, he walked to the treeline, where field met forest. "I have a favor to ask," he yelled into the forest. "I can't do this very much anymore. It hurts."

He listened, yet he heard nothing. Even the crickets had stopped chirping, but he knew that was a good thing, because that meant the ones for whom his message was meant were near.

"Now, we've helped each other out for a right good while now," Jenkins shouted into the forest. "I could have exploited you. Charged people five dollars to come see you. Sold t-shirts and coffee mugs on this new thing they call the internet, but I haven't done that." He took a pause, choosing his next words carefully. "I'm gettin' awful down in the back now," he said when he spoke again. "And I could use a little help. It's all I'm askin'."

And with that, he said no more. He limped over to his old F250 pickup, after having worked hard all day splitting and stacking firewood at the various stations he'd set up, and he drove home and fell asleep almost instantly once getting into bed.

And the next day he returned to the field to find that every single log that had been lying in the field- literally hundreds of them- had been cleanly split and properly stacked!

***

"So you're telling me," Jimmy said after 'ol Leroy had finished his story. "That you expect me to believe that you've got a couple dozen Bigfoot Sasquatches out there in your back twenty splittin' and stackin' firewood every night?"

Just as Jimmy finished speaking, the two men on the front porch of 'ol Leroy's house heard the first smack. It was the smacking sound of an ax, in a field half a mile behind the house, crashing through the first piece of unsplit, yet soon to be cleanly split, firewood. Jimmy's eyes grew big after having heard the sound, but they grew even bigger when he heard the next one only seconds later. And then the next, and then the next.

"Looks like they're startin' a little early tonight," 'ol Leroy said, glancing down at his wrist watch. It was still just a bit before nine o'clock. He'd stretched his story out a while as he'd told it, because that's what any truly good storyteller does. They stretch their stories out. "But that's okay, I guess."

"I'd best be leavin'," Jimmy said, standing and turning toward his Jeep. "I have a long day tomorrow. I'm sure I'll be bringing you out a load."

"You sure you don't wanna go out to the back twenty and have a look?" 'ol Leroy said with a smile on his face, because he knew that Jimmy was convinced. He didn't need to see.

"That's okay," Jimmy said, and he got in his Jeep without even saying goodbye, and he made his way out of 'ol Leroy's driveway and onto the main Virginia biway that would take him to Charlottesville and then home from there. He promised himself, especially after having heard such a story, that no matter how tempting it was to take a drink or twelve, he would *not* stop at the Bigfoot Sasquatch micro-brewery just down the road from 'ol Leroys.

He kept his promise.

The End

If you enjoyed this work, make sure to check out all of the other Bigfoot Sasquatch Files Volumes as well as Kevin E Lake's other books, all available on Amazon. And if you're willing to spend a little bit of your time that you will NEVER get back watching silly videos that may or may not have Bigfoot Sasquatches in them, check out Lake's YouTube channel "Homesteading Off The Grid."

Made in the USA
Middletown, DE
29 September 2020